Escape from the Deep

Contents

Written by Yvonne Cook
Illustrated by Suzie Byrne

A Lucky Escape

"Hurry, Huan! We need to get up to the next level right now! Level one is being evacuated," Huan's mother said.

"I can't find my video game," said Huan to his mother, as he tore through everything on his desk.

"We haven't got time! Leave it here. The water is already starting to seep through the cracks in the glass!" his mother shouted impatiently.

Huan looked up at the glass wall of his bedroom. His mother was right. Water was already coming in through the tiny cracks in the glass. The white pointer shark that seemed to live outside his bedroom slid past the glass of his underwater bedroom. Huan hated that shark. It was always looking in at him.

Huan had been living at the bottom of the ocean in a sea station for so long, he couldn't remember what it was like to live on land. Now, that's where he was going, to the dry world above. Huan didn't want to leave his underwater home, but they had no choice. An underwater earthquake had hit the sea station, and now it was slowly breaking up. They had to escape before the entire station was destroyed.

4

Many people had already left in submarines and headed to dry land, but with over one hundred people living in the sea station, they couldn't all leave at once.

His mother grabbed his hand and pulled him out of the room, pushing the door sensor on the way out to close the door. It didn't react, but she didn't bother to wait.

"Hurry, Huan! Hold on!" she shouted as they went up the stairs.

Level two was still safe. No water was coming in through the glass walls. How long it would stay that way, no one knew.

They heard a huge crash behind them as the glass wall of Huan's bedroom gave way to the weight of the water. Huan looked behind him. The water had already reached the bottom of the stairs. He tried to climb faster.

"Why did you have to go back to look for your video game?" Huan's mother said angrily.

She was scared. There were still a lot of stairs to the next level, and the water was getting closer and closer every second.

Huan could hear the sound of doors and walls breaking up on level one. His legs were tired, and the stairs seemed to be harder to climb than ever before. He tried to move faster, his mother pulling hard on his arm. He looked up and could see the big waterproof door of level two. It was not too far away now. They would make it.

Then it happened! Something hit Huan's foot very hard and he fell on the stairs. He didn't know what had happened.

He heard his mother scream, "Get up, Huan! Move!"

Huan was trying to move. They were almost at the door. Huan looked behind him. What he saw sent a chill up his spine. The open mouth of the white pointer shark was coming out of the water just below his feet. Now he knew what had hit him. But he didn't have time to think. He would be in the shark's mouth in a second if he didn't move!

With one final pull, his mother dragged him through the door of level two and slammed it shut. They were safe, at least for the time being.

Long Blue Arms

Huan sat next to his mother against the waterproof door on level two. He could feel the thumps of the shark butting the door behind him as the water rose. Huan had never been so scared in all his life. He looked around him at the control room on level two. It used to be full of people. Now it was empty except for Tina, one of his mother's friends.

Tina ran over to where they were sitting.

"Are you both all right?" she asked.

Huan's mother nodded wearily. She got to her feet and pulled Huan with her.

"How long have we got before level two goes?" she asked in a soft voice.

"We need to get to level three and the submarine quickly," Tina replied. "It won't be long before the water forces its way into this level."

Huan looked out of the glass wall on level two. To his surprise, the black eyes of the white pointer stared in at him.

"Quick!" shouted Huan. "We need to get out of here before it gets us." He pointed to the great white shark in front of him.

"Don't worry," said his mother, "it can't get us here."

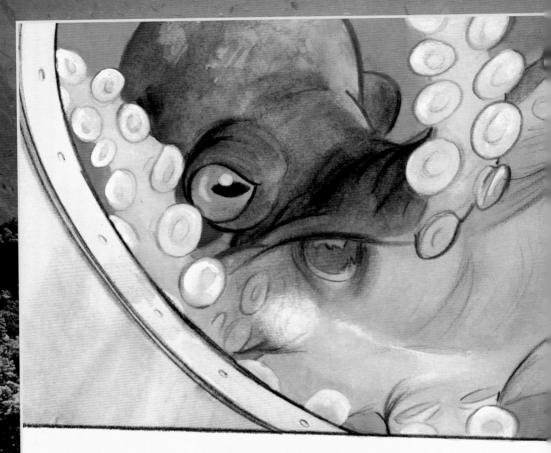

Huan wasn't so sure. He looked out the window again,
but the shark had gone.

"That's odd," he thought. "Why did it leave so quickly?"

It was then he saw some long blue arms through the glass.
They were the tentacles of a giant octopus! It seemed to be
pushing at the glass. Tina saw the giant sea creature, too.

"Oh, no," she said. "We have to get out of here. The sea station isn't strong enough any more to stand up to that giant blue octopus."

They ran to the stairs that led to level three. Huan was still out of breath. At least there was no water leaking into level two yet – but Huan was wrong.

A Fight in the Deep

Suddenly, water rushed into the room from behind the control desk.

"Run! Run!" cried Tina.

The water was coming in faster than it did on level one, but it wasn't just water coming in – long blue arms were curling in the water, reaching out, trying to grab at anything that looked like food. Huan had often seen the giant blue octopus through the glass wall of the sea station. He had often seen it grab large fish and crush them in seconds.

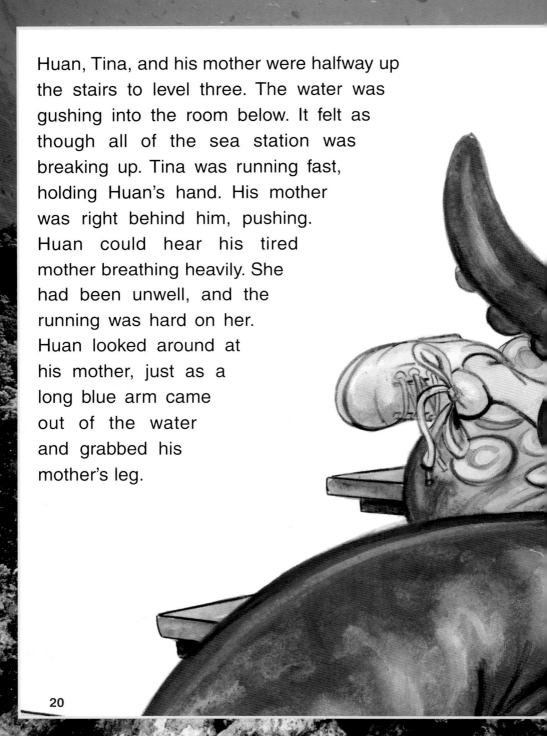

Huan, Tina, and his mother were halfway up the stairs to level three. The water was gushing into the room below. It felt as though all of the sea station was breaking up. Tina was running fast, holding Huan's hand. His mother was right behind him, pushing. Huan could hear his tired mother breathing heavily. She had been unwell, and the running was hard on her. Huan looked around at his mother, just as a long blue arm came out of the water and grabbed his mother's leg.

Huan's mother screamed. Huan called out to Tina to stop. His mother had been pulled under the water. Tina kept going up the stairs, pulling Huan's hand.

"I have to get her, Tina!" he screamed.

"We have to keep going or we'll all end up in the arms of the octopus," Tina screamed back.

Huan twisted free of Tina's grip and fell back into the water. He opened his eyes. He could see quite well. He saw his mother. A single blue arm was wrapped around her body. There was no time to think. Huan grabbed at the arm of the octopus and punched it. The arm didn't move at all. His mother was waving her free arm at him. Huan could tell that she wanted him to go.

Huan lifted his head above the water and took a breath of air. When he went back under he could see another blue arm. It hadn't grabbed his mother yet, but Huan knew it would soon. He could never break the hold of two octopus arms. Quickly Huan did the only thing he could think of – he grabbed the arm of the octopus that was wrapped around his mother and bit it as hard as he could and kept on biting.

At first nothing happened, but suddenly the octopus let go. Blood flowed into the water from where Huan had bitten the creature. His mother was free, but Huan knew that they didn't have much time. He was sure the octopus wouldn't give up. Huan's mother had lifted her head up above the water and was swimming to the steps. They could hear the octopus thrashing in the water behind them, but they didn't look back.

As they reached the stairs, Huan could see Tina and a man standing at the open door on level three. The man was holding out a long pole.

"Grab the pole!" Huan heard Tina shout.

Huan and his mother grabbed onto the pole and Tina and the man pulled it to them as fast as they could. Huan could hear the blue arms thrashing about in the water right behind them, just as the man grabbed them both and pulled them through the door. Tina pressed the door sensor. The door started to close, but the blue arms were still coming. They were almost to the door, and the door was still not closed!

Through the crack in the door, Huan could see another visitor. The shark was back. This time it wasn't interested in him. It was after the bleeding arm of the octopus. Huan watched as it opened its great mouth and bit. Another arm rose out of the water and lashed at the shark. The shark dropped under the water. The door closed. Crash!

Escape from the Deep

Huan looked at his mother. She was clearly unwell, but she looked at Huan and smiled.

"Thank you for saving me," she said.

"We've no time to lose. The station's breaking up fast," Tina said. "Come on!"

Tina was right. The water was already seeping through the door. The man helped Huan and his mother to the submarine waiting at the level-three port.

They moved as fast as they could. Huan could still hear the water behind them. He knew it would break through at any time and flood level three. Then there would be no escape. They would all die!

The door of the submarine was right in front of them now. Huan, his mother, and Tina fell through the open door and onto the soft seats of the submarine. The man closed the door tight.

Huan looked through the window of the submarine. They were safe. He heard the engine of the submarine start and felt it move slowly away from the level-three port. The sea station was a sad sight, a broken tangle of glass and steel.

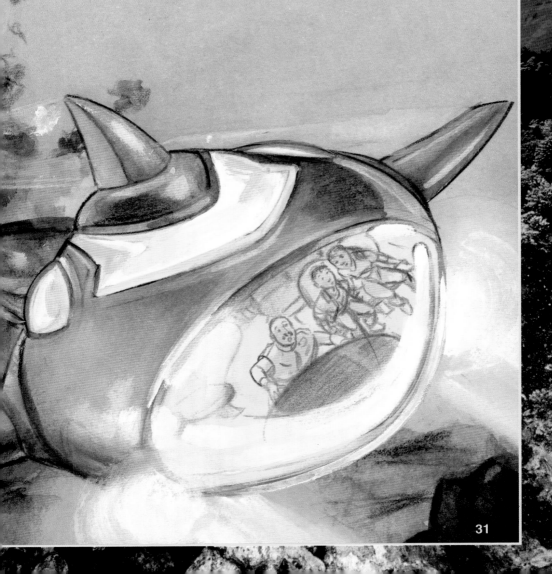

The submarine moved quickly through the water. Huan wondered what happened to the giant blue octopus and the great white shark. He knew he would never find out. What Huan did know was that some day he would live below the sea again. He looked across at his mother sitting in the seat next to him. She was asleep. Huan closed his eyes and thought how lucky they had been to escape from the deep.